The Wonderful World of Disney

Walt Disney
CINDERELLA

Twin Books

DERRYDALE BOOKS
New York

Once upon a time, a lovely girl named Cinderella lived with her evil stepmother and her two vain stepsisters, Anastasia and Drizella. The stepmother made Cinderella her servant, and forced her to sleep in the attic.

One morning Cinderella's bird friends
awakened her with a song. She and Jaq,
the mouse, stretched lazily and thought
about what a nice day it would be.

The morning quiet was soon shattered, however, by the shrill voices of Cinderella's stepsisters, demanding breakfast. Cinderella dressed in a hurry and rushed to the kitchen, where she scarcely had time to cook before her stepmother summoned her with a bell, ordering the poor girl to clean the house.

Meanwhile in the royal palace, the king complained loudly to the grand duke. "The prince must find a bride!" he proclaimed.

The grand duke suggested that a ball be held at the palace, and that all eligible young women in the kingdom be invited.

The king was delighted. "Issue the invitations immediately!" he exclaimed.

The very next day a
messenger arrived at the
house where Cinderella
and her stepfamily lived.

"By royal decree," he
announced, "a ball will
be held for the prince, and
all eligible young women in
the kingdom are required
to attend."

"Could I go to the ball?" Cinderella asked hopefully. Her stepsisters laughed at the thought, but their mother said slyly, "Of course you may, as long as you have something to wear."

Cinderella's mice friends,
hiding in the candleholders,
overheard the conversation.

The mice also overheard the stepmother's plan to keep Cinderella too busy to make herself a dress for the ball.

Anastasia and Drizella ordered Cinderella to wash their clothes, sew their dresses, scrub the floor and do other chores.

The mice rushed up to the attic. Jaq explained the stepmother's evil plan to Gus and the other mice. "We can't let this happen!" he exclaimed. "Cinderelly will never have time to make her dress."

The mice had an idea: They found a dress that had belonged to Cinderella's mother, and with help from the birds, they began to restyle it.

The mice and birds cut the fabric and sewed on ribbon and pretty trim. They found a lovely necklace for Cinderella to wear. When the gown was finished they all admired it.

When Cinderella came to the attic, she
was surprised and grateful. "Oh, goodness!"
she exclaimed. "It's a beautiful gown. I'll
be the happiest girl at the ball! Thank you!"

But when Cinderella's stepsisters saw her dressed up for the ball, they flew into a rage. "Look, mother! She's stolen my necklace!" screamed Anastasia, ripping the jewelry from Cinderella's neck. The ugly stepsisters grabbed at Cinderella, and in moments her gown was in tatters.

The stepsisters and
stepmother left for the ball,
and poor Cinderella ran to
the garden. She sobbed as
her animal friends sadly
stood by.

Suddenly she heard a kind voice. Cinderella looked up into a lady's friendly face. "Who are you?" she asked.

"I'm your fairy godmother," the lady replied. "And I will grant your wish to attend the ball."

To Cinderella's amazement, the fairy godmother quickly went to work with her magic wand. She transformed a pumpkin into a coach, Cinderella's torn gown into a beautiful new one, the horse into a driver, the dog into a doorman, and ...

... the four mice into four white horses. Cinderella thanked her fairy god-mother, then she stepped into the coach.

The horses pulled the handsome coach through the countryside. Cinderella thought about her fairy godmother's departing words. "You must return by midnight," she had said, "because then the spell will be broken, and everything will be as it was."

When the coach arrived at the palace, the guests gazed at it in wonder. Cinderella still could not believe her dream had come true. She took a big breath and stepped out of the carriage. Glowing with happiness, Cinderella entered the ballroom.

The prince was overcome by Cinderella's beauty.
Immediately, he asked her to dance.

The handsome couple swirled to the music, as all the royalty and all the young women of the kingdom admired their grace. Cinderella's stepsisters and stepmother looked on jealously. They did not recognize her.

Cinderella and the prince danced again and again, growing more fond of each other as the evening passed. Suddenly the clock began to chime, and Cinderella realized it would soon be midnight. She dashed away from the prince.

"Oh no!" she cried, rushing into the waiting coach. The coach sped away, and it was then that Cinderella realized she had lost one of her glass slippers as she ran. The clock continued to sound as she raced toward home.

Suddenly it was midnight, and the spell was broken. The mice, the horse and the dog turned to look at Cinderella, who sat in rags on the pumpkin.

The next morning the king summoned the grand duke. "The prince wants to marry the lady he danced with last night," he said, "but he doesn't know who she is. Take this glass slipper to every house in the kingdom until you find the one it fits. She is the one he will wed."

When the word spread, Cinderella's stepmother ordered her daughters out of bed. "Hurry!" she demanded. "Out of those clothes and into your dresses! You still have a chance to marry the prince."

Then the evil stepmother, who knew in her heart that Cinderella's beauty far surpassed that of her own daughters, quietly climbed the stairs to the attic.

The stepmother opened the door. "The king's messenger is coming to find the young woman who lost her glass slipper at the ball," she told Cinderella. "He won't find you!" And before the girl could speak, her stepmother slammed the door and locked it.

"Oh, please!" cried Cinderella. "Don't lock me in!" But her stepmother slid the key into her pocket and went back downstairs, ignoring Cinderella's pleas.

Soon the grand duke and his servant arrived, bearing the glass slipper.

"It's mine!" squealed Drizella.

"No, it's mine!" shrieked Anastasia.

Jaq and Gus hid in a
teacup, waiting for a
chance to get the key.

In the meantime the servant tried to fit the tiny slipper on Drizella's large foot. "It fits me perfectly!" she exclaimed, even though only her toes fit. "You just have to push a little harder."

The servant pushed and shoved.

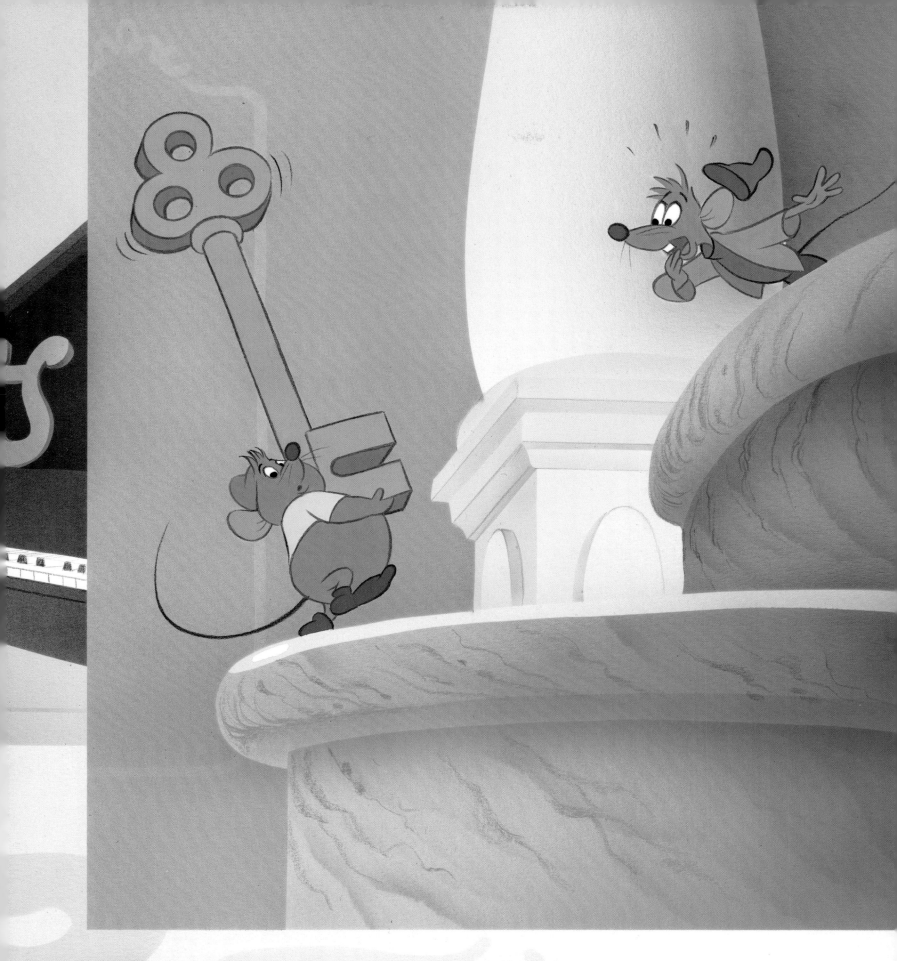

 While the stepmother watched her daughters, the mice
snatched the key out of her pocket. They began hoisting it up
the stairs to the attic.

Gus would hand the key
to Jaq, then climb onto the
next step, where Jaq would
hand it back.

Finally their efforts were
rewarded. They reached
the top step and slid the
key under the door.

In the meantime, Drizella had finally wedged her foot into
the slipper, to the grand duke's utter dismay. He didn't think
she would make a very good princess.

But since he was under orders, he began to proclaim that the prince's bride had been found. Drizella's mother beamed with delight, imagining herself living in the royal palace.

Suddenly the slipper popped off Drizella's foot. The servant tried to catch the slipper, but it sailed over his head ...

... and smashed to the floor.

"Oh, my!" exclaimed the grand duke. "How will we ever find the prince's bride now?"

Just then Cinderella rushed into the room.

"Why, I have the other slipper here,"
she said, handing it to the grand duke.
He snatched it up with a smile.

"Let me try the slipper on your foot, young lady," said the grand duke. When Cinderella was seated, he slid the slipper onto her foot. The duke was as delighted as Cinderella's stepsisters were horrified.

"Hooray!" shouted Jaq. The mice
danced about gleefully.

Soon wedding bells rang throughout the land as Cinderella and the prince were married. Everyone came to the wedding — except Cinderella's stepfamily, who refused to attend.

Since Cinderella and the prince were very much in love, it was a happy wedding indeed. Their eyes shone with joy as they pledged their wedding vows.

No one attending the wedding was more pleased than Gus and Jaq, who congratulated each other for playing a part in Cinderella's good fortune. Together with Cinderella's other mice friends, they moved into the palace, where they and the royal couple lived happily ever after.

This 1988 edition published by Derrydale Books, distributed by Crown Publishers, Inc., 225 Park Avenue South New York, New York 10003

Directed by HELENA Productions Ltd. Image adaptation by Van Gool-Lefevre-Loiseaux

Produced by Twin Books 15 Sherwood Place Greenwich, CT 06830

Printed and bound in Hong Kong

ISBN 0-517-67010-0

h g f e d c b a

The Wonderful World of Disney